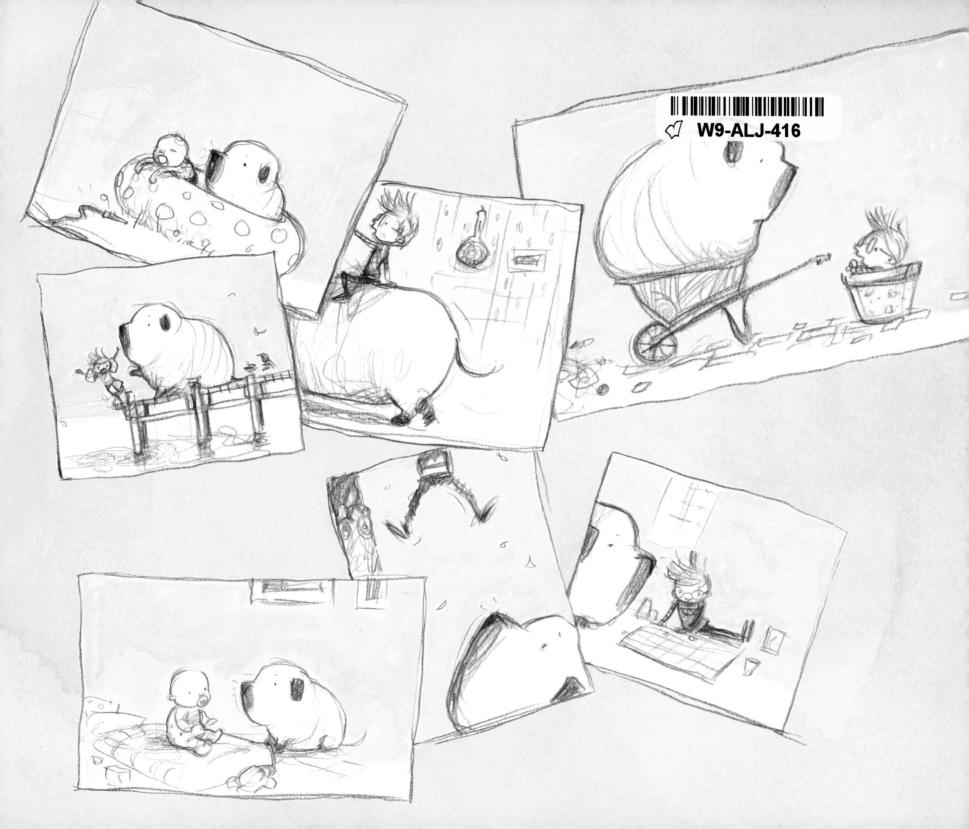

For Lacie and Bry—the two dogs that inspired Augustus

First U.S. edition 2020
First published by Walker Books Australia 2019

Library of Congress Catalog Card Number pending
ISBN 978-1-5362-0967-9

25 24 23 22 21 20
CCP 10 9 8 7 6 5 4 3 2 1

Printed in Shenzhen, Guangdong, China

This book was typeset in Handwriter.
The illustrations were done in watercolor, gouache, and pencil.

Candlewick Press
99 Dover Street
Somerville, Massachusetts 02144

visit us at www.candlewick.com

Ollie and Augustus

Gabriel Evans

CANDLEWICK PRESS

Ollie was small—like a pickling jar or a shoebox.

Augustus was big—like a fridge or a table.

They did most things together:

painting,

bike riding,

Giraffes sleep standing up.

people watching,

dressing up,

To the Bikemobile!

digging

(Ollie's favorite thing),

tree climbing,

and stick collecting

(Augustus's favorite thing).

Sometimes Ollie was annoying.

Sometimes Augustus was irritating.

Sometimes they got mad,

but they usually made up by lunchtime.

One day, everything changed.

Ollie had to
start school.

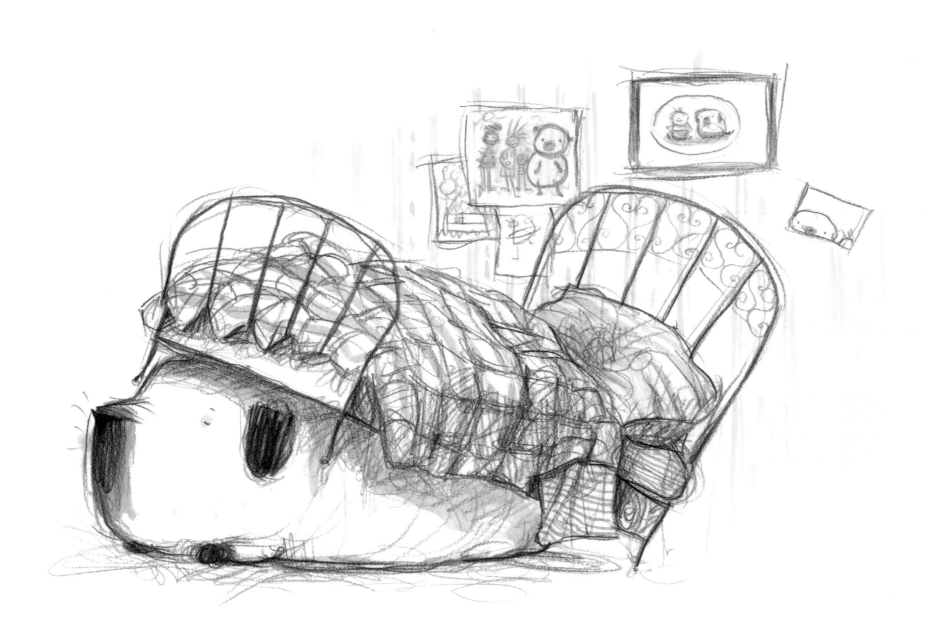

He was worried that Augustus would be lonely.

Ollie had an idea.
Wanted: Friend for Augustus.

Augustus has a fun,
outgoing personality.

He enjoys long walks
in the park,

weekend trips to the beach,

watching sunsets
over a bowl of
water,

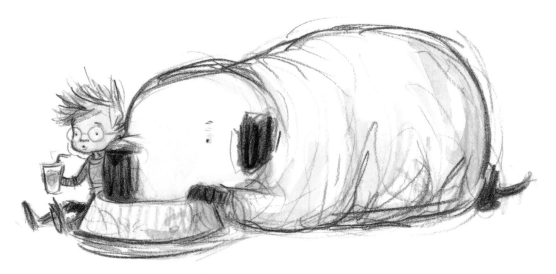

and Friday nights at home.

Henry, I'm leaving!

Looking for a dog with a sense of humor, similar interests,
and a passion for stick collecting.

The next morning, dogs were lined up at Ollie's door.

The first playdate wasn't successful.

Neither was the second.

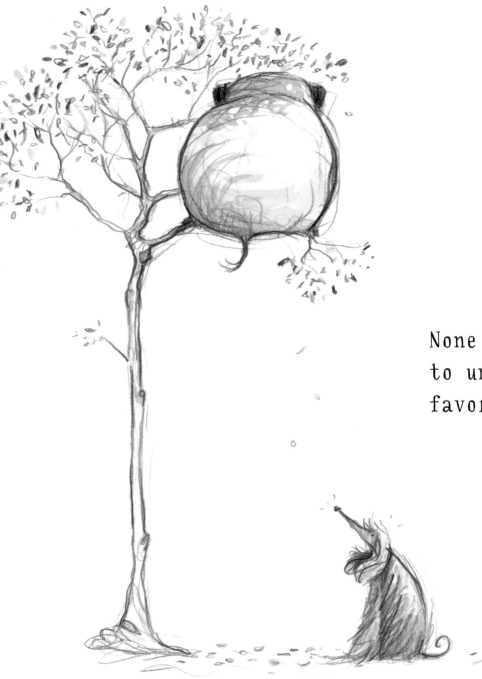

None of the dogs seemed
to understand Augustus's
favorite things.

Forgive me,
Henry.

And Augustus didn't understand their interests:

tail chasing,   licking,   howling,

shedding,   sniffing,

or fetching.

Worst of all, they didn't understand
Augustus's appreciation of sticks.

Ollie was sad.
Augustus would be lonely.

The next day, he went to school.

He worried and worried.

Augustus did not.

He had plenty to do.

And he knew that Ollie would always come home . . .

with exactly what he needed.